The TOOTH FAIRY LOSES a TOOTH!

by Steve Metzger Illustrated by Ailie Busby

LITTLE SIMON

New York London Toronto Sydney

It happened early evening—
it really is the truth.
While chewing on a bagel,
the Tooth Fairy lost a tooth.

"Oh, my!" she called out with surprise. "One bite was all it took."
She flew up to her mirror. "Hey, check out my new look!"

"Now that my first tooth is out,
I have a wish in mind.
Right under my pillow,
I hope that I might find . . .

a coin or a tiara . . .
a dress that's red and frilly . . .
a lollipop or storybook . . .
A kitten? That's too silly!"

As the Tooth Fairy flew away,
the wind blew through her hair.
"When I return," she sadly sighed,
"my tooth will still be there."

"If only I was just a kid like other girls and boys.
I would get some money—or perhaps a brand-new toy."

"It's just not fair!" she grumbled.
"I travel every night
to the homes of children
while they are sleeping tight."

"If someone would leave a gift for me,
I'd be really glad!
But no one will remember me,
and that just makes me sad."

Around the world the Tooth Fairy flew.
She didn't make a peep
giving treats to boys and girls
who were fast asleep.

When she finally finished,
she said, "My work is done!"
While flying through her window,
she saw the rising sun.

She tiptoed to her pillow. She raised it just a bit.
Finally she took a look. Then she had to sit.

"Oh, my! It's bright and sparkly.
I don't believe my eyes!
A fairy has remembered me.
What a sweet surprise!"

"I was not forgotten. I'm as happy as can be.
Someone thinks I'm special . . . and really does love me!"